This book is dedicated to my brother Fin.

This is Fin when he was little.

This is Fin now with his pet chickens Maggie and Rosie.

This is fin

and this is fin's GINORMOUS pet giraffe.

or so he wished...

Mum and Dad
thought animals
were SMELLY
So Fin was not
allowed a pet.
SO
instead they gave
him a
STUFFED
crocodile to play
with !

The problem was, Fin was an only child
So he wished for a pet to go on adventures with...

So one day Fin came up with a
BRILLIANT idea.

He would BORROW some
animals from...

his SCHOOL
FARM!!!

Later that day, Fin RAN home and
hid the ants under his bed.

Fin thought he had got away
with it, so he went out to play.

But all of a Sudden...

Fin heard MUM bellowing his name!

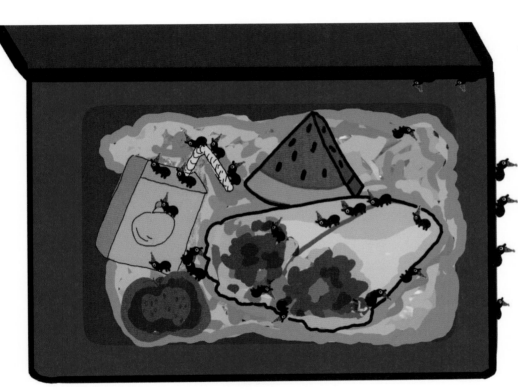

There
are
ANTS
crawling all
over
your
lunchbox!

"Maybe I need something
that isn't going to escape
so easily," wondered Fin...

So that evening at bath time, Fin came up with a
great idea.

AND GUESS WHAT MUM AND DAD FOUND THE NEXT DAY...

well there
were
3 rats
last time
Fin checked!

Two SMELLY rats and a SUPER long snake!

So the next day, Fin put ALL the animals BACK!

BUT...

when Mum and Dad checked the next day, they found...

Phew! That was close, thought Fin. As his parents hadn't seen

the

slimiest
snail

sliding
its way

up his
lunchbox!

The
End

what animals would you sneak in your lunchbox?

Printed in Great Britain
by Amazon

79488748R00016